Timesong

Timesong

by Bill Branon

illustrations by Dwain Seppala

Huntington Press

Huntington Press
3687 South Procyon Avenue
Las Vegas, NV 89103
(702) 252-0655 Phone
(702) 252-0675 Fax
lva@las-vegas-advisor.com Email

Timesong © 1998 Bill Branon

Cover design: Jason Cox
Production: Jason Cox
Interior design: Bethany Coffey
Cover illustrations: Dwain Seppala

1st Edition—March 1998
ISBN 0-929712-54-4

…for Gladys, my mother

Author's Note

A book like *Timesong* flows out of the past, not the present. I've spent sixty years on this earth. Twenty-three of those years were spent putting Marines and sailors back together...and identifying the remains of those who were too broken. I've spent my time in church as an altar boy. I've spent my time at Harvard with the pitchmen of science. Then, a decade after college, on the sponson of a Navy ship in the middle of the Pacific beneath a night sky so deep that I had to hold on to the rail to keep from falling up, I came to the crossroad we all come to. Religion or science? Who to believe? A tough choice. I now realize that a choice wasn't necessary. In the words of j.b., *Timesong's* coyote, "...they are hunting the same rabbit."

After reading *Timesong,* those readers who enjoy extrapolating a book's premise are invited to ponder: (1) For a specific human, 'me'-time must be continuous, there can be no interval between 'me' lifetimes. (2) Awareness is the goal of evolution. (3) If God is universal awareness, as most religion and much of philosophy profess, does it not follow that He must revisit His own evolution? (4) As science wanders into the realm of that first fractional nanosecond and comes eyeball to eyeball with theology, possibilities blossom. Even the Big Chill option may not negate the premise—the Big Bang occurred once, why not again?

On a technical note, I'd like to respond to a well-read friend who wondered, "In light of the fact that suspension of disbelief is pivotal to a work of fiction, how do you expect any reader to accept the premise that a coyote can communicate with an autistic child?" May I offer this: If you can tell me how an autistic six-year-old, without any piano training, can play thirty minutes of Mozart after hearing the piece only once, and play it perfectly, then I shall explain to you how an autistic child can communicate with a coyote. …I'll buy the beer.

Timesong, in some respects, resembles a children's book. That decision was deliberate. The format was chosen to invite young minds…and old eyes. But *Timesong* most certainly targets the sophisticated reader; mixing scientists and saints is heady business. My hope is that this little story might ease at least one child past the inevitability of loss…even if that "child" is eighty years old.

The author is indebted: To Anthony Curtis and Deke Castleman of Huntington Press whose editorial expertise and willingness to roll the dice on a different table gave life to *Timesong*. And to the staff at Huntington whose enthusiasm and skill are evident in their product—Len Cipkins, Bethany Coffey, Jason Cox, June Flowers, Jacqueline Joniec, Jim Karl, Michele Bardsley, and Deanna O'Connell…you're part of the nicest surprise I've had this year.

To Art Flowers (Anthony's dad) and to Virginia Castleman (Deke's wife) who were drafted into service…you know how to make rough rock smooth.

To Lou Boxer in Philadelphia who refuses to let me take a break from writing, to author Bob Holt for his friendship and energy, and to Kathie Harrington in Las Vegas whose poignant twenty-six year journey with an autistic son puts the word 'love' in perspective…you are all special to me.

To my wife Lolly and my mother Gladys, both of whom have decided in the past few years to challenge the abilities of cancer surgeons. I thought heroes were born, not made. I was wrong.

To family and friends who give me pieces of their heart. You wrote *Timesong*. I just punched the keys.

And, last but not least, to my "other" publisher who

told me *Timesong* wouldn't fly: I hope you're wrong, but even if you're right, without you, I wouldn't have met the gang at Huntington. That was a special favor.

My gratitude to all.

A day will come when beings...shall stand upon this earth as one stands upon a footstool, and shall laugh and reach out their hands amidst the stars.

—H. G. Wells, *The Discovery of the Future*

I

*T*he shape moved down from Ice Mountain in that coldest hour before dawn. It ghosted across the flatland beneath dying stars. No rock scraped and no twig snapped to mark its passage. Coyote. Male. Young but fully grown. A silent passage...more remarkably silent because the animal moved on three paws. The lower half of its front left leg was missing.

j.b. crossed a black road, then grass, and lay down on red stones beneath a dark green bush near the side of the library. The high wall sheltered the coyote from marauding slivers of north wind. He rested and watched night go to early-morning gray. Dawn crept into a low sky. Orange streaks ignited inside long blue clouds like embers being fanned to life by the breath of a rising sun.

As he waited, he thought of the time of the pain.

He had stepped into a steel foot trap when he was a yearling, when he was still careless and too curious. It had been the scent of man that had made him paw at the leaves covering the trap, a scent that should have been a warning, not an invitation. But curious was what he was about. And that curiosity had nearly done him in.

His mother had come in the hour of the pain and had chewed off the snared leg to free him from the cruel steel jaws. She carried him by the nape of his neck as she had done when he was a pup, carried him to a place high on Ice Mountain where cold water took away the hurt, made the bleeding stop, and let him live. And it was she who stood between him and the others after she brought him back to the cave, she who bared her fangs, ruffed her fur, and fought three days to stop the pack from enforcing the law that says a mouth that doesn't hunt is a mouth that should not eat. They had finally accepted his difference…at first, only because of her, but later because of him when he began to show that, despite his missing limb, he could contribute.

j.b. had come to realize that the time of the steel trap, as terrifying and painful as it was, had been an opening, a dangerous opening, but an opening nevertheless.

The steel trap had made him different. And because he was different, he was special. He *had* to be special.

Soon after the sun lifted above the dark ridge, he saw them. The boy with the mother. Humans. Walking as they did each day at dawn before the cars and trucks and workers came. Walking even before the people with the dogs came, dogs that seemed happy on lengths of rope or chain despite the perversion of such a thing, dogs that marked small trees with urine and growled at one another from the safety of the leash.

He watched the mother and the boy come toward him on the wide sidewalk that circled the library. Soon they would be near the red stones where, as on each morning, she would stop and pretend to look at something else as the boy moved away from her into the green bushes to be with the coyote.

The boy was not like other human children that j.b. watched in the schoolyard or at the food places. The boy had a different gait and cocked his head to one side like a sage hen. At times his upper body bobbed up and down like a reed stalk dipping in the summer wind.

The two humans came to the red stones. The boy walked through the bushes. He squatted down next to j.b., and something like a smile came onto his face as he reached out and touched the young coyote.

j.b. looked at the mother standing alone on the sidewalk many steps away. She was nervous and kept looking from side to side to see if anyone was coming. Letting her son approach a wild animal might be an irresponsible thing to do in the eyes of others, but the coyote was his light, the only thing that brightened the shadows of his day.

_____

She was a good woman of great intelligence in the world of humans, a teacher and forensic scientist, but she carried a burden that scrambled her gift of logic in a skillet of fear: her boy Tom, autistic, incapable of communication and hopelessly dependent in a world that could not help and would not listen. His sudden fear of death after the funeral of his father, her dear husband Ross. The desperate tantrums. The sullen isolation. It had been a mistake letting Tom go to the funeral. Until that day there had been improvement, some small victories. But now? She had no answers, no answers where answers had been her pride. Her hours fused, one into the other, like melting cubes of ice; cold hours lost in the numbing chill of love unable to find a way.

So full of questions.

So empty of answers.

The two of them, mother and son...

...so alone.

"Hi, Tom."

"Hi, j.b."

"Any luck, Tom?"

"No. I can't make the sound of their words. I just can't."

"That's too bad," j.b. said.

"I wish there was a way."

"Me, too. I'm sorry, Tom."

"It's hard to be different, isn't it j.b.?"

"Yes. Very hard."

Midnight. j.b. crouched low. Human shapes, outlined by tongues of flame from the fire pit, moved back and forth. There must have been twenty of them. They drank what they called beer from cans, and their sharp yells hurt his ears. The shouting of the humans didn't build music the way his pack's hunting howls built music. The hard noises made the front of his head itch, and he twitched his nose several times to make the itch go away.

He concentrated on the smell of meat stacked in slabs on a wooden table away from the fire. The aroma made the inside of his mouth run wet.

Wait. He would find a way. Wait.

No moon drifted in a sky left to stars. The land was defined only by fire shadows and by the irritating human

sounds that made all creatures silent.

He stayed directly downwind, although he knew from long observation that such precautions were unnecessary. Humans had absolutely no ability to track scent. Not these by the fire, not the ones at the food places, not even Tom. None of them. And yet, they were so many. Surely, their numbers would not last.

His chance came when a male and female climbed onto a flat rock and began to gyrate on their hind feet to a terrible noise coming out of a black box. The others circled around, made slapping sounds with their front paws and chanted like winter loons.

j.b. seized the moment and snatched three large steaks from the wooden table.

The distance back to the cave was considerable. With the heavy steaks clamped in his teeth, the three-legged coyote moved over the land, a shadow crossing shadows. He stopped a few times to rest. But j.b. did not eat any of the meat. Not one bite.

When his mother saw him returning, she yipped. The Leader emerged from the depth of the cave. For j.b., it was a supreme moment. The Leader was usually hunting when j.b. got back with forage, and the moment of j.b.'s coming-in was always lost in time.

Perhaps the Leader was not hunting because he was

sick. Or his bones were hurting from the cold. Or something else…j.b.'s mother said the Leader was coming to the changing time. Maybe that was it.

Later, when the others returned, the Leader stopped the carriers from regurgitating the deer kill for the pack. Instead, he indicated they could keep the kill in their stomachs, that the unfed ones would have enough from j.b.'s contribution. With his snout, the Leader pushed one of the steaks toward j.b.

In turn, j.b. chewed the steak in half and nosed the larger piece to his mother. It was easy to share the bigger "half" with someone he loved as much as he loved her.

Then, on three legs, with pride, he ate.

II

Heaven and Earth are as old as I,
and ten thousand things are one.
—Chuang Tzu, China, 300 B.C.

"Hi, Tom."

"Hi, j.b."

"Your eyes are red. Did you get sand in them?"

Tom's body rocked back and forth more than usual...and he craned his neck repeatedly. j.b. could see that Tom was having a difficult time. "No," said Tom, "I was crying. I had a bad dream."

"What did you dream about?"

"My dad, about my dad. About when he went away."

"Where did he go?"

"He..."

j.b. waited.

"He died. He's never coming back. I didn't want him

to die. He would hold me. He would sing to me before I went to sleep, and I would put my head on his chest and feel his voice rumble inside him."

"Die? What does 'die' mean?"

"It means gone forever."

"Gone?"

"Yes."

"Forever?"

"Yes."

A car came toward the library. Tom's mother saw it coming. She called, "Come on, Tom. It's cold. We'd better get going." As always, she was afraid that someone would come along and see Tom with the three-legged coyote, afraid that someone would laugh or say something mean, afraid that someone might think the coyote sick or dangerous and harm the animal. She didn't want that. The walks to see the coyote seemed to be the last door to the outside world, to reality, to normalcy. She would keep that door open.

Tom moved away, heading back to his mother. "Good-bye, j.b.," he said over his shoulder and, reaching her, grabbed her hand.

Die? thought j.b. and cocked his head to one side, trying to understand.

Seven months earlier, when j.b. was very young, he found out something amazing about the humans. The discovery happened on one of his foraging trips to the place with the yellow curves. Despite their pitiful, almost embarrassing lack of survival characteristics—slow of foot, no scent-tracking ability, total ignorance of the necessity to properly mark territory—the humans had, nevertheless, developed a surprising knack for scratch talk, what they called "writing." j.b. had to admit that they were good at that. Very good. Of course, the pack had no need for such a thing. The pack communicated perfectly well as it was. There wasn't a need for extensive scratch-talk development. Quite unnecessary.

j.b. made his discovery in the large trash bin next to the yellow curves. It had been right there waiting for him. He had a special liking for the thing humans called "cheeseburger." Cheeseburger had a milk curd melted on meat. It tasted so fine, like the milk he once took from his mother mixed with the meat he ate now when the pack came in with fresh road kill. But everything was all jumbled up in the trash bin, and the smell of fire-burn was all over the place. That made it difficult to find cheeseburger by scent alone. What he discovered was that humans always made certain scratches on the papers that were wrapped around the milk-meat parts. The scratch marks were always the same for cheeseburger. Other foods also had their own particular scratch marks. It didn't take long to associate different scratches with the different types of food inside the colored paper.

Not if you were really hungry.

j.b. learned "hamburger" and "fish sandwich" and "milkshake" and "Big Mac." "Big Mac" had green leaves of plant mixed in, a thing he didn't go for. He was purely a cheeseburger kind of fellow. It wasn't long after that first discovery that j.b. learned to associate the sounds humans made with the different types of scratch marks. It was easy.

Especially after he discovered the secret passage in the place the humans called "library."

j.b. was returning from an unsuccessful twilight foray to the place where the big garbage trucks went too fast around a sharp turn. But nothing had spilled out. There were no bones to collect. Because of the cold wind, j.b. sought shelter in the lee of a large building made of cinder stones.

Behind a bush he found a place where warm air blew from a hole in the wall of the building. The slatted cover had fallen off the hole and lay on the ground. The warm air felt good, especially on a cold October night. Dark and mysterious, the black hole made him very curious.

He looked around.

No one.

Curiosity had nearly been the end of him more than once. But it was warm in there. And that hole, where did it lead? Whose den was it? Was there food inside? What made the heat come out? How far in did the hole go? He looked around again. No dangers. Not even a recent human scent on the earth close by. Only the spoor of a rabbit. And two ground squirrels.

j.b. ducked through the opening. He stopped and listened. The tips of his claws made odd clicking sounds on the bendy metal floor of the cave. The surface was slippery beneath his paws, but there were ridges and bumps every few feet to give him a grip, and he had no trouble navigating after his eyes became accustomed to the darker dark.

The warm wind moving through the duct felt so good that it made his ears tickle. The hole seemed to lead way back into the building. If there was one thing j.b. liked to do, it was explore.

He spied a light ahead. It came from a grate in the side of the tunnel.

j.b. edged closer to the light and peered out. Below him and sitting around a wooden table were seven pup-humans and one she-adult. They had scratch-mark packets in front of them on the table. All the packets were the same. Each page had a picture of something familiar to j.b., and under each picture was a bit of scratch talk.

"Open your books to page three, children."

The packets were called "books" by the humans.

"What is that a picture of?…Anyone?"

"A tree," from a she-pup.

"That's right. A tree," said the adult.

j.b. knew trees.

"And how do we spell 'tree'?"

Small fingers pointed at each piece of scratch talk. "...T...R...E...E," the pups said together.

"That's right, children. Very good."

j.b. didn't miss a class. Six weeks. Every evening. Peeping through the grate. Lying in his secret spot where sweet warm air whispered through the metal cave. Scratch talk was quite easy once you got going with it. Especially if you were good at shapes and could remember. Like all coyotes, j.b. was good at remembering. And he was real good at shapes. It was his special gift.

There was something else, too.

j.b. discovered that the metal cave was made up of many different tunnels. The passages led everywhere, and j.b. was able to look into almost every room in the library building. Sometimes, when there were no scratch-talk classes for the pup-humans, j.b. would spend his time investigating the tunnels. He found places where he could look through other grates, places where adult-humans gathered in packs and listened to leader-humans who would talk about books. Sometimes, the same human who made the book was there to talk, and that gave j.b. a special thrill. But what j.b. liked most was when the humans did what they called "poetry." He liked the sing-song chant of poetry. The fit and rhythm of the sound was like the talk of his own kind. There was meaning in the rhythm.

j.b. was proud of what he learned about the humans. It was a coyote's job to learn. Like the way his mother taught him about where water hid in caves during the hot summer, about how the wind came from different stars as the seasons changed, about the way ants and bees and deer and cougar gave directions to their own kind. These things were useful. Strength grew from learning.

j.b. knew that humans also recognized the strength of learning. They certainly spent a great deal of time jabbering about things. And the books, that was probably a pretty good idea, after all. But my goodness! Human ideas were so confusing. There appeared to be no central truth in their conclusions. Too much knowledge, too little truth. It seemed to j.b. that the humans were so set on just talking that they often forgot what they were talking about. When a simple truth appeared in their words, it was often lost in "what ifs" and "back-minding." j.b. had been told by the Leader about back-minding. Back-minding happened when you twisted the obvious. Like when you knew the rabbit you were chasing had taken the path where the thorn bushes grew, but you insisted on hunting the path that ran through the shade by the brook because it was easier and you could run faster.

j.b. would listen at the grates in the library walls and marvel at all the different thoughts. He learned more and more about the humans, about things and places he had never seen or been told about. Not by his mother, not even by the Leader. The cave called "library" proved to be a place full of wonder and discovery. Despite the humans' aptitude for astounding distortions and irritating back-minding, j.b. could tell from pictures and from the human speak-leaders that the world stretched far beyond the End Mountains.

He could see why Tom was having such a difficult time. There were so many ideas in the human world, so many choices.

Perhaps confusion came because human heads were too big. Too-big heads probably had too many thoughts inside. That might be it. A too-big head probably caused all sorts of problems.

Poor Tom.

The night after Tom told about his father going away, about the dying, j.b. lay with his mother on the western slope of Sandy Mountain. They watched valley shadows come out to hide from moonbeams.

j.b. rolled onto his back and flailed about, scratching, stretching, and playfully flipping sand at his mother. She did not growl. When he was through, he lay next to her so their sides touched, and together they watched the night crystallize as day-dust settled down.

Quiet moments passed.

The land began to sparkle as shy bits of quartz and timid flats of mica started to flirt with stars. Without looking at his mother, j.b. said, "The humans…I know what their word 'die' means, it means 'the changing.' But they are made too sorrowful by it. Maybe it means something more to them."

j.b.'s mother was silent. She watched a far rabbit flicker between moon shadows. Then she said, "Maybe it means something less to them, j.b."

III

Know that the world is uncreated, as time itself is, without beginning and end.
        —The Mahapurana, India, 9th Century

"Where did those come from, j.b.?"

"From the place with the yellow curves."

"And again you got them from the humans?"

"Yes," he replied.

"The Leader will be pleased," said the mother.

The young male coyote moved past her to the rear of the shade cave. His forage of two half-eaten hamburgers lay on gray stones at the cave entrance. j.b. had gotten better at working the high school lunch crowd at McDonalds. It beat trying to get into the tall metal trash bin after midnight. He licked his whiskers and discovered a tart fragment of pickle stuck to his upper lip. He couldn't dislodge the piece with his tongue and, because he was missing his front left paw, he was forced to crouch down on his chest and use his right paw to pry the morsel off. He chewed the piece. The pickle-taste made his eyes water, but the flavor was strong and nice.

"Why don't you eat one of these, mother? The Leader will not know there were two."

"j.b.!"

"But you need more food."

"Don't say such things. The pack is nothing without community. You know that. It's our strength, our way."

"You're the only one I care for. The others ..."

The mother snorted and bit j.b. on the neck. But not too hard. And j.b. did not yelp. "Why are you so different?" she scolded. "How long do you think any of us would live without the first law? We hunt together. We share kill and share forage. Always! It is the order of things and the reason the pack is ageless. Why do you say as you do? Why do you have to be different?"

j.b. turned his head so his mother could nuzzle and lick behind his right ear. It was a spot he couldn't scratch because of the way he was, because the front leg that should be used to support his weight for ear-scratching wasn't there. She always helped him clean behind that ear. It was their ritual. The warmth of her tongue and the firmness of her grooming made him feel like a pup in the summer sun, and his eyes closed in sleepy pleasure.

Later, when the rest of the pack returned with only two lean jackrabbits to show for the long night's hunt, j.b. was not there. The Leader ate the two hamburger pieces while the others nibbled on rabbit carcass. The Leader looked at the mother. His hard yellow eyes acknowledged j.b.'s forage. He looked into the shadows of the cave.

"Where is j.b.?" he asked.

"j.b. is by the building with the red stones."

"There is no food there," said the Leader.

"I know," said the mother.

"What are you doing, Tom? Where's your mother?"

"I hooked her to the bed, j.b. I just hooked her to the bed."

j.b.'s eyes went wide. "You mean you trapped her to the bed? Made her be caught in a trap? You couldn't have done that, Tom! Not that!"

"I did too!" Tom sat on the ground by the dark green bush near the red stones. He bent his legs up and wrapped his arms around his shins, a thing that j.b. could not do. Tom squeezed his arms tightly and tried to make himself into a little bump on the earth. His head began to bob up and down, but he kept his eyes on j.b. all the while and made the eyes squinty and dangerous looking.

"But Tom! Her leg! She might have to have her leg chewed off!"

Tom changed his squinty eyes, made them real eyes again, then looked past j.b. at a distant nothing. "No," he said. "I didn't trap her leg. I trapped her arm."

"Why, Tom? How?"

"Handcuffs."

"Handcuffs?"

"She got them from a man. She was going to put them on me. She said so last night when I broke stuff. The man, the next-door man, he said she should put handcuffs on me if I broke stuff." Tom's head bobbed with more energy.

"I don't want that. I don't want that! So I hooked her to the bed. I hooked her to the bed when she was sleeping."

"Handcuffs. What are handcuffs?" j.b. had a quizzical look. He didn't know handcuffs. "Do they break a bone? Do they make blood come? Do they make pain?"

"They are not like what happened to you. They only hold you to something. They are holding her to the post on the bed. They don't make blood come."

"Can you get her out of the cufftrap?"

"I can if I want to."

"What do you mean…'if you want to'? And how do you get her out?"

"I could undo her. There's a key. But I don't want to."

"A key? A thing called 'key' makes the trap let go?"

"Yes."

"I wish we had a key. For the pack to use. A key would be a very good thing to have, very good, indeed…for us."

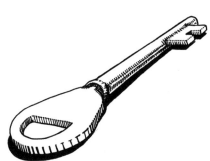

Tom looked at the sky, then back at j.b. He shook his head. "I didn't bring the key with me. I left it on the table in the kitchen. Besides…"

"Besides what?"

"She'll probably yell for the next-door man to help her. He works at night. He comes home pretty soon. Yes, she'll yell for him to help. And he'll undo her."

"Will you be bitten, Tom? Scratched? Because you trapped her? Will you not get forage to eat?"

"I don't know."

"What do you want to do? Where will you go?"

"I'll go with you. I'll go where you live."

j.b. laid his ears back. "I don't think so, Tom. You're different. You aren't like us. It would be all right with me, of course. I like humans—you, the young people at the place of the yellow curves who give me cheeseburger—but the others, the pack, they would not accept you."

"I'm not so different. I'll be a friend. I can help."

Now it was j.b.'s turn to make squinty eyes. "I couldn't be there all the time. I have to forage. I have to explore. You'd be lonely."

"I know how to be lonely."

j.b. thought for a few moments. He cocked his head to the left. He cocked his head to the right. Finally he said, "Well, we'd better do *something*. The sun is waking up. Soon people will be here. Come, we'll go to Ice Mountain where the cold water is. We'll find out what has to be done. I'll ask my mother. I'll ask the Leader. Perhaps they will know what to do."

"This is a high place, j.b."

"Yes, Tom. It's a very high place."

"And the air is cold."

"Let's rest in the sun awhile."

Tom looked around. He saw a honeycomb in the crook of a short tree growing in a split rock nearby. "j.b.! Bees! There are bees here. They'll sting us."

"No, they won't sting us."

Tom sat down next to j.b. and watched the bees moving on the face of the honeycomb. "Look how they move, j.b., look how they move. They seem so busy, so confused."

"They are always busy."

"Do bees talk? Do you know what they say? Can you talk to bees, j.b.?"

"I can't talk to bees, Tom. But I know what they say." j.b. scrunched forward on his belly so his nose was next to the honeycomb. Tom stretched out on his stomach next to j.b. "See that bee that's coming in to land, Tom? Watch what he does."

Tom saw how the bee walked slowly in a tilted figure-eight pattern.

"That bee has found food, perhaps a pretty mountain flower," said j.b. "He's telling the other bees where the flower is. If the flower is nearby, he walks in a small round circle. If the flower isn't so near, he walks in a flat circle that would be tilted in the direction of the flower. If the flower is a long way off, the bee makes a figure eight and walks very slowly like he is tired from the long flight. That's what he's doing now. And see how the figure eight is tilted? That shows where the flower is from the sun. He's telling the other bees where the flower is."

Tom smiled. Then a look of excitement came to his face. "Look, j.b., look! Those bees are flying off. They're going where the bee came from! How do you know these things, j.b.? How do you know about the bees?"

"Well, I just know. Bees are part of the mountain, part of the flatland, part of everything. You can't know the mountain if you don't know the bees. Knowing is the best thing to do."

"But I don't see how you know about bees. Did someone teach you about them?"

"We learn from others or we learn alone. It's all together. It all counts. And little things count as much as big things. Little things help to know about big things."

j.b. and Tom went farther up the mountain. j.b. showed Tom a cave. The cave was deep and dark.

"This will be a safe place for you to stay for a while, Tom. No one lives in this cave. When the night comes, go way in the back and lie next to the rock. The rock remembers the sun. It remembers the sun all through the night. Stay close to the rock. I'll be back tomorrow. I'll find out what we should do."

"I'm afraid."

"Don't be afraid."

"What if a bear should come?"

"A bear? No bear will come." j.b. couldn't resist a comment. "If you had a better nose, you'd know that."

"What is there to drink?"

"The rocks back in the cave will give you water. It's

good water, clean water. If you're quiet you can hear it dripping." j.b. remembered a picture he had seen in a book at the library. He remembered a word under the picture. "Make a cup with your hands like humans do when they do the thing called 'pray.' You can catch the water that way."

"Is there anything to eat?"

j.b. snorted and made a coyote smile. "Eat? Well, Tom, there's honey to eat. Don't you remember? I'll bring some to you in the morning."

"j.b.!"

"But I had to make him safe, mother."

"You know what will happen, j.b. The humans will look for him. They will come to Ice Mountain. They'll look into all the places we live and may find us. There will be great danger."

"Will they come right away?"

The mother thought for a while. "Not right away. They'll probably look among their own kind first. And in the flatlands. But they will come. Not right away, but soon. Perhaps in two days. Or three."

"I can't *make* him go back, mother. I can't drag him. He's too big."

"I know that." She thought for a longer moment. "Can you make him *want* to go back?"

"I don't know."

"Can you make talk with him?"

"Yes, mother. He remembers in shapes. Like I do. He does his numbers that way and makes sound shapes on a thing called 'piano.' He told me about it. That's the only time the humans listen to him. But that isn't important now, is it?"

"No, j.b., not now. Now you must study him, ask him questions, find out what's wrong. You have to make him want to go back."

"I will try. Poor Tom," said j.b.

"Poor *Tom*?" A coyote tear came as she thought of Tom's mother.

IV

In those days came John the Baptist preaching in the wilderness…and his meat was locusts and wild honey.
—Matthew 3:1-4

"Do you like the honey, Tom?"

"Yes. It's good. How did you get it from the bees without getting stung?"

"It's not hard. Not when you know how. The cold morning makes the bees slow and sleepy." j.b. stretched out on the dirt in front of the cave. "I like to discover things, Tom. Like how the bees are. Do you like to discover things?"

"I like to discover things. But I only discover small things that aren't important. You know how to find food. That's important. I discover things that don't count."

"You told me how you discover sound shapes on the piano box. You said it makes your mother and other humans listen, makes them smile and talk. You make them happy.

Doesn't that count?"

"No. It doesn't. It's a little thing."

"To make them happy is a little thing?"

"Maybe it's not so little. But it doesn't make *me* happy."

"…I heard about it from my mother. It happened before the pack came to this valley. It was in the time of the great winds."

"I would not like to see your pack kill a lamb."

"The storm gave us no choice."

"And that's why the men hunted you? Because you took their lamb?"

"There was more than one lamb."

"When the Leader's son got trapped, why didn't its mother chew off her son's leg like your mother did to save you?"

"I don't know, Tom."

"Why did she just stay there by the trap with the Leader's son? Why didn't she run away when the hunter came?"

"I don't know that, either."

"You said she just sat there and got shot?"

"The hunter shot them both."

"Do you think your mother loved you more? To chew off your leg, I mean?"

"I don't know, Tom…"

"I wish I could talk to them, talk to other people, talk to my mother. I'm so different."

"Being different might be a good thing, Tom, even if it hurts sometimes. Being different makes you think real hard, like when you touch fire. Don't you think so?"

"I guess." The boy reached over and absently put his hand on j.b.'s paw.

"Thinking mixed with hurting really stays with a fellow, Tom."

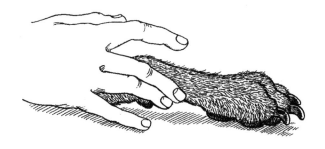

Down on the flatland a swirl of dust appeared and danced between stalks of mint-green sage. The swirling funnel twisted and turned and played with sticks and spun small leaves into the sun.

"Look at that, j.b.!"

"I see it. You humans, what's your name for it?"

"That's a dust devil. That's what we call it. What do

you call it, j.b.?"

j.b. moved his paw and rubbed his whiskers to remove some bits of sand stuck there. "That's leftover coyote." Tom looked at j.b. and saw a coyote smile wrinkle j.b.'s nose. "The Leader says that when a coyote goes from life, something stays behind…something that holds on for a little while until we have a chance to say goodbye. He says there's always something left after each life no matter how small the life is. Some of the others don't believe the Leader about that. They think the Leader is making a story. But they don't let him know that they don't believe him."

"Do you believe him, j.b.?"

"Yes, I believe him. All coyotes know about the changing time, but some coyotes…well, that's as far as they believe."

Tom watched the dust devil dance along a hunting path that wound through the flatland. "What do you call dust devils, j.b.? You must name them something."

"Angels."

"What do you think your mother is doing now, Tom?"

Tom stared at the ground. "I don't know."

"I'll bet she won't ever think about putting a cufftrap on you again."

Tom didn't speak.

"She won't try to tell you what to do anymore."

Tom didn't speak.

"You showed her you can do what you want to."

Tom didn't speak.

"You showed her that you know just as much as she does."

Tom didn't speak.

"You showed her."

"You'll get tired," said j.b.'s mother. "Hunting at night, being with the boy during the day, not sleeping. You must do something. The other humans will come soon."

"I can't find a way. And I can't leave him."

"You have to try, j.b."

"Something is holding him back. Something stronger than being with his own kind. Something that will not let him see."

Under a quarter moon and lying by a hole in a fence, j.b. waited for the dog on the other side to be let into the house for the night.

j.b. fell asleep.

Falling asleep near the fence was dangerous because the dog, after burying a superb dinner bone two hours ago, kept coming back to check on it. Each time he would come to check on the bone, he'd pass close by j.b.'s spot. Big dog.

Probably too big to get through the hole in the fence. But you never could tell.

j.b. would get that bone.

If the dog didn't get him first.

j.b. had watched this one before. He had been behind the fence so long that even when the single gate on the far side of the yard was left open the mutt didn't have enough sense to go through it. The dog thought his world ended at the fence...and so it did.

A short time after dozing off, j.b. woke with a start. He scrambled to his feet. The dog, finally seeing him, barked once and charged. And ran into the fence. And fell down.

Silly dog.

But j.b. didn't care. He moved away on quick coyote feet into the silent shadows of night.

j.b. had realized something.

Something more important than the buried dinner bone.

V

Why, what could she have done, being what she is?
Was there another Troy for her to burn?
      —W. B. Yeats, *No Second Troy*, 1910

The library was mostly dark. Only a dim light showed behind the big glass doors, and j.b. could see the wooden desk where, during the day, the humans went with their books before taking them out of the building. Nothing moved inside.

j.b. went to where the vent cover lay on the ground behind the bush. He sniffed the air. He looked around. He entered the tunnel.

Deep into the building, back where the warm air was almost too hot, j.b. came to a place he had found a week ago where a grate hung loosely on hooks. When j.b. first discovered the grate, he had been surprised to find that if he pushed at the grate with his nose it swung up and, when he stopped pushing, it swung back into place. None of the other grates did that.

  j.b. pushed the grate open. Below him in the dark he saw a ledge of small white ponds. He knew they were ponds because he had seen water running into them when the human he-pups used them to put water on their paws after marking other small ponds along the far wall with urine. The air smelled very sharp. The he-pups certainly knew how to mark.

  Although it wasn't much of a drop to the white ledge,

j.b. slipped when he landed on it, and he tumbled onto the floor. He fell, not only because he had three legs instead of four, but because the white ponds were hard and slippery like mountain ice. Claws didn't work on the pond ledge any more than they worked on ice. It took a full minute for j.b. to stop hurting. And he didn't feel much better after the hurting stopped because returning to the tunnel now seemed a very difficult thing. Maybe impossible. The ponds were too slippery to stand on. How would he get back up to the grate?

He'd have to figure that out. Later.

For now, something more important needed doing.

He left the room of white ponds through a door that was held open by a stick with dead grass on one end. He proceeded down a dark hall.

j.b. stopped and stared. In the soft light of the place he couldn't believe his eyes. Incredible! Coyotes! Four of them! Two adults. Two pups. Standing right in front of him. Staring right at him!

He laid back his ears, cocked his head to one side, and pulled his tail down between his legs, submissive, their territory, their place, he the alien.

They didn't move.

He crouched lower. Laid down. Rolled over.

Still, they didn't move.

He waited. And waited some more.

They seemed frozen. No tail twitched. The eyes were flat.

The four silent ones were there, but not there.

j.b. got up. He moved toward them. He stepped over a small ledge and walked on sand that didn't squeak, walked on grass that wasn't cool to his paws, walked past twigs of sage that were too brittle.

The four *had* been coyotes…his kind…but were no more.

What had happened to them? j.b. shivered with curiosity.

Then he backed off, turned, and went to look for the things he had come to find.

Security guard Reno spun around, her hand on the weapon in the holster on her belt. She listened. Not moving.

A second noise!

The dull thud of something falling. A book.

There had been incidents of vandalism recently, valves broken on the pumphouse by the reservoir, words spray-painted on the highway bridge, a break-in across town at the new school. She carried a pistol because she had been told it would scare away burglars. She had been told that acting tough was important.

Once again a sound came from the row of shelves near the auditorium.

She didn't turn on the overhead lights. Out came the big pistol from its holster. She'd catch them by surprise. They wouldn't know she was there. But the weapon made her more afraid. Maybe it was too heavy. It trembled in her left hand. She needed more time to think. She didn't think well when she had to think quickly.

She looked small inside the uniform she wore.

A scraping sound. Something moved to her right.

Courage stumbled. So did she. Her elbow bumped the edge of a metal shelf. The sound to her right stopped.

More fear.

The pistol's hammer, cocked by her thumb, clicked into position with a gentle, ear-splitting clack.

No more sound. Now they knew she was there for sure! Beads of sweat huddled along her spine and drew a tell-tale line on the back of her guard shirt.

Suddenly, something scurried across dark corners, suddenly darker. She spun in that direction. Whatever it was, it was running toward the east wing where the restrooms and offices were located. She began to walk after it. The motion of her pursuit made her bolder. She walked more quickly.

She followed the scurry at a trot now, followed it all the way back to the end of the building where there was no light. A brave thing for her to do.

Then something happened that stopped her heart. Behind her, out of a dark recess in the wall, a recess she had

41

passed short seconds before, the thing she chased bolted back the way it had come. A grunty gasp of fear escaped the throat of guard Reno.

She swallowed terror and willed her unwilling legs to move again. She started back toward the center of the building. The thing she chased had gained considerable distance.

The sound ahead went to nothing. Guard Reno stopped, stood very still, and listened. Silence as cold as lost hope hovered in the empty hall.

She took one step forward. Then another. Three more. She walked with tick-ticking heart and tiny breaths, walked with pistol drawn and finger slippery on the steel trigger, walked inside her uniform toward the thing she knew was waiting.

She entered the small rotunda that separated the children's reading section from the main room where books for adults were kept. The rotunda contained the wildlife exhibits: the birds, the snakes, the animals. So many eyes. Each eye looking. Each shadow waiting.

Guard Reno stopped and listened. She did not inhale. She saw the reaching claw of branches with the mighty snake wound around…saw the thin silver wires that pinned unmoving birds onto a painted sky…saw the haunting desert scene with its five coyotes staring into velvet silence.

And nothing moved except her fear.

After a few stark seconds more, she allowed one breath, just one, then moved out of the rotunda into the wide hall that led to the front of the building.

Guard Reno spent a fitful night; she worried each long minute into every endless hour and wondered, more than once, if she had seen what she had seen and heard what she had heard.

In the orange splash of dawn, after the first desk worker came and guard Reno left for home, after the first pot of morning coffee bubbled in the administration office, after the doors that could see things coming and open by themselves were turned on, a small shape moved out of somewhere. It made the seeing doors swing apart by jumping up and scampered out across the white sidewalk into the new day, a pair of books held tightly in its teeth.

VI

Modern physics and chemistry have reduced the world to an astonishing simplicity: three elementary particles put together in various patterns make, essentially, everything.

—Carl Sagan, *Cosmos*, 1990

j.b. dropped the books onto the sand. "Tom? Are you awake?"

After a short moment, a sleepy Tom, rubbing his eyes, appeared at the cave entrance. "Hi, j.b." Tom blinked in the morning brightness and yawned. He squinted cautiously at the sun as if it were something to be wary of.

"Did you sleep well, Tom?"

"Yes."

"Wait here. Make yourself awake all the way. I'll get some berries for you to eat. Would you like a bit more honey from the bees?

"I still have some, j.b.," said Tom, "...from yesterday." Tom looked at the two books and yawned once more. "What are those for?"

"For us. I'll be right back. The berries are close by."

While j.b. foraged, Tom turned pages. He could read, but it wasn't something he often did; reading made him ache inside because he couldn't form the sounds writing intended for human ears.

One of the books had a yellow cover. The word "Atoms" was written there above a picture of a small boy looking at dots and circles. The other book had pictures of planets and swirls of stars. It was a thin book, not big at all. On pages in the middle, Tom saw pictures of the man the story was about. A man called Stephen Hawking. The man was crippled, twisted, frail. Tom could see, as the pictures went along, that the man, growing older, became even more crippled. The last pictures showed the man in a wheelchair, all slouched over and very thin. *He is melting*, thought Tom, *He is different. Like me. Like j.b.* But in spite of the wasting away, there was, in every picture of the man, a smile so real and eyes so full of life that Tom smiled back, a thing he had never done to a picture in a book before.

j.b. came back with berries on a stalk.

They sat on sand still cool from the night and ate sweet berries in the morning sun.

"These are good," said Tom. "What kind of berries are they?"

"We call them locust berries," said j.b.

"I did not know there were things like berries and honey and water up here."

"There are things everywhere we do not see," said j.b. "It's a matter of knowing how to see, I guess. Don't you think so, Tom?"

Tom wiped berry juice with his sleeve.

They rested and watched as the rising sun made small shadows out of big shadows on the flatlands far below.

Then j.b. said, "Tom, your father did not die, he only changed."

The words startled Tom. They came from nowhere. Sharp words, though softly said. Tom felt his chest begin to hurt inside. He didn't know what to say. *Why do you want to make me sad?*

j.b. saw tears glisten.

"Can I tell you about your father, Tom?"

Tom's look was angry then. A tear ran down. He glared at j.b. In Tom's mind the shapes began to tumble. He could feel the rage come as it always did when confusion dissolved into frustration. His head began to bob.

"You better not get mad at me, Tom. I'll go away." Stern words.

"It was a nice day. So nice. The berries are good. Why did you spoil it?"

"Tom, you're acting like a pup. I'm sure this is important for you."

Tom glared again.

"I'm sorry if I made you angry," said j.b. Soft words now. "Do you think I want you to be angry? Do you think I want to make you sad?"

Tom wiped a tear with his sleeve. It was the same sleeve he had wiped berry juice with, and a red smear lingered where the tear had been. He stared down at the sand. The rage began to sink back; the shapes began to settle.

"Nobody's perfect, Tom. I only have three legs. The Leader can't answer all the questions. My mother doesn't know how to get cheeseburger from the place with the yellow curves. And you humans have too-big brains. Too-big brains make you look past answers. It's not your fault. That's just how it is. Everyone has things that aren't right. That's what 'special' means. It's sort of funny, Tom, but being different is the only thing that makes us all the same."

j.b. sat down on the sand close to the boy.

"One night, when I was in the library…"

"Library? You were inside the library?"

"Yes. I've been inside many times. I know a way to get in, but that's not important. As I was saying, one night I was there after most of the humans had gone. I went farther into the place to listen to a scratch-talk leader make words to a pack of adult-humans. She talked about the things of the night sky and about the thing you call time and about the pieces we are made of. Particles, atoms…those were the words she used. Those were new words for me. Particles. Atoms. I'm always glad to learn new words." He licked his whiskers. "And there were strange light-pictures on a wall. It was the light coming through the grate that drew me to the place at first."

j.b. paused and looked at Tom. "Have you ever seen the light-pictures on the wall?"

"Slides," said Tom.

"Slides?"

"I think you saw slides. We have slides at my house. My father is on the slides at my house." Tom began to look sad once more.

"Your father…" And j.b. nuzzled the other's hand with his nose so he would not be upset. "…that's why I'm telling you this story, Tom. You said your father was gone forever. You said he did a thing called 'die' and 'die' was forever."

Tom only nodded and put a quiet hand on j.b.'s back and buried small fingers in the animal's soft fur, a gentle touching.

"I think that what you call 'die' hurts you too much. The mind-pictures of your father make you sad." He waited, then added, "You don't understand about 'forever,' do you, Tom?"

"I want him to come back, j.b."

"He *will* come back."

The boy looked at the coyote, then looked away. He did not believe.

"I am only a coyote…but you are only a human. We know, the whole pack, we all know about the changing time. It comes to us with birth. It's not a thing the Leader has to teach. It simply is. But it's not the same for you, for any human, is it?"

Tom only listened.

"At first I didn't realize—your not knowing, I mean." j.b. pushed at the boy's hand again to make him listen. "Your father—he's not gone. He *will* come back to you."

"How can he come back? He *can't* come back. He'll never hold me. He'll never sing to me again."

"You're wrong."

Tom's hand fell away from j.b.'s back. "He is gone."

"He is not gone."

"Yes, he is!" Tom pounded on the sand with his fist. "You're talking about the slides, about the pictures. That is not 'back.' I want him really back! So I can touch him."

"You will be able to touch him."

Tom made a horrible face. "You talk like the church people do, j.b. You talk about make-believe things. You're a fat liar!"

j.b. struggled hard to keep from growling at Tom. This was not going well. He tried to calm the boy by changing the subject a bit. "I know your 'church people.' I like them.

I've heard them talk in the library. They are close to seeing. But sometimes they get silly and snap at church people from other packs. Why do they do that, Tom? Why do they do that when most humans don't even see at all?"

Tom ignored the question. All the shapes were beginning to tumble again. "You're making everything come apart, j.b. Sometimes I don't like you! Why don't you just go away?"

The coyote got up and walked over to a small bush and marked it. With his back feet he kicked lots of sand around. After several long moments of serious sand-kicking, j.b. came back and stood directly in front of the boy.

Tom rubbed at another tear.

51

"I'm not asking you to believe. I'm only asking you to listen." The words still had an edge to them. j.b. took a deep breath and muttered, "Now I know why my mother nipped my ears when I was young." His eyes softened, and he sat again where he sat before, next to the boy.

"Please just listen to me, Tom. Okay?"

No reply. But no more name calling.

"The thing that's strange," said j.b., "is that the answer's right in front of you. It's in this yellow book the pup humans use." He put his paw on the small yellow book, the one with "Atoms" written on the front. "And it was in the words of the people who talked about time and particles that night in the library. But they missed it. In all the big words, they missed the little words."

"What little words?"

"The words that say three things. The words that are not 'church people' words." He bit at a flea. "Last night, when I was trying to steal a bone from Big Dog, I thought of a way. Make the yellow book go to twelve, Tom."

"Twelve?"

"The pup-teacher told the pups to open to twelve."

Tom opened the book. Two lines of big-letter words and a picture were on page twelve. He read the first line: "Everything is made of particles that last forever." Tom glanced at j.b., then read the second line: "The particles separate and come back together to make new things."

"Don't you see, Tom? The particles change into new things…the changing time. That's what happens when the thing you call 'die' happens. 'Die' *is* the changing time. But the biggest word in all those words is 'forever.' I don't think you humans know what forever means…not really."

"I know what forever means."

"You have to be careful with 'forever,' Tom. Forever is more than 'big.' Big doesn't even work with forever." He watched a yellow butterfly land on the boy's shoulder. "You don't need church-people talk if church-people talk bothers you. Just those three things: Particles…that mix…forever. You have to scrunch up your brain a lot, but you can get it if you try."

"This is very hard thinking, j.b. I'd rather eat berries."

"You can eat berries later!" j.b. twitched his ears several times, and Tom could see that he definitely didn't want to eat berries. "…Particles that mix forever. Your 'particle people' take a long time to learn, but now they know. That's why I got the books. One of the reasons. So you could see I'm not making up stories."

Tom wasn't looking at j.b., but he was listening hard.

"The Leader says that because of 'forever' everything that was will have to happen again. You can't die, Tom. Your father can't die, either. None of us can. We can only change. Sometimes the parts, the particles, make a tree, sometimes a star, sometimes you and me, sometimes your dad again. It goes on and on. The changing doesn't stop. Ever. It *can't* stop."

The butterfly flew off Tom's shoulder. With his sharp coyote eyes j.b. saw how the soft wings moved tiny swirls of air.

"My dad can happen again?"

j.b. cocked his head and made a teacher-face. "Make believe you have a pile of stones. Three white stones, three black stones, and three red stones. You put them in a line. Now close your eyes, mix up the stones, and make another line. Do it over and over. Pretty soon you'll make a line exactly like the first line…" j.b.'s brain was starting to hurt. "…The stones are like our particles. Somewhere in forever, you'll *have* to be just like you are now. But you have to think hard about forever. Forever is the very hardest part."

Tom interrupted, "Forever is a long time."

"These are real things, Tom. Not make-believe things. Not things that make some humans wrinkle up their face because the words sound like church-people words. It's numbers. Just endless time and numbers."

"My dad will come back?"

"Yes, he'll come back. Sometimes he'll die like he did this time, and sometimes he won't die like he did this time. These things *will* happen. It never stops. Someday you'll have him back. Really back."

"Oh my, j.b."

"Oh my, yourself, Tom."

"I guess I won't know about all this when I come back?…what you just said? So I'll have to hurt?"

"Some of those times you'll hurt and some of those times you won't hurt. Some of those times I'll be here and some of those times I won't be here."

"That won't be good…if you're not here."

A coyote smile. "The Leader says that's why it's important for us to think about how we treat each other now. He says that in another time we might be on the 'getting done to' side instead of the 'doing to' side."

j.b.'s eyes filled with a strange, soft light. "That's what comes with being part of forever, Tom. 'Die' isn't the problem. Maybe *not* being able to die is the problem."

"You said our bodies come back, j.b. And you said before that there's something left over, like the dust devil, the angel."

"That's what I said."

"But what about me? I'm a 'me.' I'm something in between. I'm not just a bunch of parts and I'm not just an angel. I'm a 'me,' the things I do, the things I know, the things I feel. What happens to me? Does 'me' come back?"

"The 'me' stuff is real hard, Tom. The Leader doesn't think that the 'me' is important. He thinks a 'me' is just the feeling an angel gets when it's stuck to a bunch of parts."

Then j.b. squinted one eye at Tom. "But I'll tell you

a secret. *I* think about the 'me' sometimes, too. Do you think that if all the parts go back exactly the same way, and they have to, sooner or later, well, do you think that the 'me' could be the same again? Do you think it could happen that way?"

Tom made a big-thinking face. "I think maybe it *would* be the same, j.b."

"You could be right, Tom."

"These are hard things to decide."

j.b. turned to look out across the flatland. "Maybe not too hard." Without looking back at Tom he said, "Have you ever been in a place you've never been before but you feel like you've already been there?"

"Maybe a couple of times."

"The Leader says our 'me' remembers little pieces of other times when things were exactly like they are now. Do you think he could be saying a true thing, Tom?"

"I don't know."

"Time is the key, Tom. The Leader says that time isn't like a hunting path, not a straight line. He says that time is more like the morning mist. It's all around us. That sometimes we see things in the mist that have been like before."

They watched a hawk carve circles in the sky.

And then they ate berries.

A new look came into Tom's eyes. "Then why are we here? Why are we here at all?"

"I don't know, Tom. All I know is that you were being hurt too much by the thing called 'die.'"

"But I want to know more, I want to know why we are."

j.b. made a coyote sigh and looked at Tom. "I fix the 'die' thing for you and now you want more?"

"But I have to know. Why are we here if it's just numbers?…if it just keeps going on and on, over and over?"

"Greedy he-pup."

Tom put his hand on j.b.'s back again. He pinched j.b.'s skin, but not too hard. "Tell me what you think about the 'why.' Tell me."

j.b. looked down at the flatlands where the day's first dust devil skittered through the sage. With a movement of his head, he made Tom look where he was looking. "That something left over after each life? The angel? The Leader says it comes here to learn about love and pain. He says that *what* happens to us is mostly up to chance…but *why* things happen to us is as real as rock."

"What do you think, j.b.?"

j.b. waited a long moment. Then, "Once, when I was small, on a day when I was too bold because the pain in my leg was big, I asked the Leader why I had to hurt so much. He said that the body uses pain to teach the angel important things…like cold rain teaches winter seed to make flowers."

j.b. smoothed his whiskers.

"The Leader could be right," he continued. "He's close to the changing time. He says that the changing time lets us see 'forever' right in front of us…like a tree or a stone."

"A thing to touch, j.b.?"

"Yes. He says the changing time is when our angel goes back into 'forever'…like a raindrop on the river…but only after the angel learns about love and pain. Angels have to know these things, I guess. They just have to."

j.b. bent his head and licked sand off the stump of his missing leg. "The funny thing about humans," he added, "is that it looks to me like the 'church people' pack and the 'particle people' pack are hunting the same rabbit."

j.b. was silent while he and the boy watched a white bird fly low across the flatland below them. Tom smiled. He had never looked down on a bird flying.

"If you really have to push it," said j.b., "and remember, all this 'forever' stuff is new to me, too…I mainly do cheeseburgers…well, I think something does come of it. Something that lasts in a new place."

j.b. looked at the boy and said, "I can't say I understand all of it. Maybe the angels are building the thing you humans call God…

"…but what do I know? I'm only a coyote."

VII

"Everything trembles, as if the World, well-ordered world, were trying To disintegrate itself back into Chaos and Night, be formed anew. Keep your heart for me, and one day we shall meet again..."

—Goethe

She pricked her ears forward, raised her nose, and worked the air. She had been near the library before, but only once...a time when she came to see how j.b. got so close to the human mother and her boy, the one j.b. called Tom. She had not crossed the road that day, but had remained on the flatland at a safe distance. Watching. Testing for scent. Recording in her coyote brain the shape and motion that characterized both humans. It had been a thing done as much out of curiosity as out of concern for what j.b. was doing so deep inside the alien world of man.

Now, she would use what she had seen. She picked a hole in the dawn and flashed across the black road into the green bushes by the red stones.

She was so afraid.

But fear was less than love.

The sun was close to the edge of East Mountain. The smell of dog was not far off. The coyote knew the human mother would start each day here. It was the logical place to start, the only place to start.

She hunkered down on red stones and waited. In the distance, at the edge of the black road, she saw a shape in motion. Memory matched stride and carry. The boy's mother was coming toward the library.

The female human stopped. A full-grown female coyote stood before her on the sidewalk, the animal trembling, fighting panic, looking every way in each moment, but standing there. Waiting.

Coyote eyes looked into human eyes.

The coyote spun in a tight circle, then took four quick steps west toward the mountain...and halted. The human did not move. The animal spun again, walked west, waited.

Tom's mother made three tentative steps toward the animal.

The coyote backed toward the mountain, stopped once more.

A pickup truck came toward the library from the east and slowed.

The female coyote held her place, her eyes wide with hot fear. Animal eyes pleaded with human eyes for understanding.

Finally, the human followed, cautious at first, then more quickly as the coyote moved west.

Back by the library, the pickup slowed, then stopped. Two men got out of the vehicle.

"Look at that, Edwin! Over there! That coyote. And that woman. Isn't that the lady who lost the kid? The ones in the pictures that are posted all over town?"

The beefy man squinted through a small set of binoculars lifted out of the cab. "I think you're right, Abbott. It sure looks like her. That coyote must be sick. Else it wouldn't be close in like that. Maybe it's got the rabies. Maybe it got the kid. Maybe it just went after her. Get the rifles. Get 'em quick."

The thin man reached into the cab of the pickup.

"Tom! Look! It's your mother coming!"

"Where, j.b.? Where? Your eyes are better than mine. Where?"

"There. The shadows by the broken rocks. And look…my mother! That's *my* mother in front of her."

"Are they coming here? Are they coming to the cave?"

"Oh yes, Tom. They're coming here. There will be four of us to eat honey and berries together for awhile…before she takes you back…before your mother takes you back." j.b. put his head up and gave the hunting "come" howl. The joyous sound echoed off rock, spilled into the wilderness, laced the air with a brilliant, haunting noise.

Down by the broken rocks the female coyote stopped at j.b.'s howl. She answered, her reply deep and strong. It carried the sound of power, of a hunt hard-won and finished. She had brought the woman, the mother. The pack would be safe. The men and yellow dogs would not come to look for the boy. But she howled for something more. She was a mother, too.

The big female coyote backed off the hunting path. Tom's mother had seen the shapes high on the cliff when j.b. howled. The morning sun painted the two young ones in sharp relief against the steep gray wall of rock, and they were easy to spot.

j.b.'s mother let the human female pass by to go to

her boy Tom. No need to get closer to the human. j.b. might do that kind of thing, but not her, not with the acid aftertaste of fear still in her throat from being too near the place called library.

She watched Tom's mother start the climb toward the ledge, then turned and started back down the south trail. There was one more job to do before she could go back to the place where her pack slept in cool shadows. She had seen the glitter of reflected sunlight on blue steel as she led the human mother to Ice Mountain. Two men. They must be turned. They must not find j.b. and the boy. The men would not understand. They must be turned.

j.b. and Tom sat side by side and watched Tom's mother pick her way between the boulders that lined the narrow dirt path leading up Ice Mountain.

"j.b., why isn't your mother coming up?"

"I don't know. I thought she would. Perhaps there's something more important."

Tom got to his feet and slowly began to back toward the opening of the cave.

j.b. turned his head to look at the boy. "Tom? Where are you going?"

"She'll be mad at me. For what I did." And he disappeared into dark shadows.

j.b. turned again to look down at the path and yipped a sharp yip so that the woman would know, in all the confusion of rock, which ledge to head for. He knew by now that it was more than likely that humans with their too-big brains couldn't remember simple things like which ledge was which. Then he got to his feet, shook himself, and moved into the cave.

"She'll be mad."

"She loves you, Tom."

"She'll put the handcuffs on me." Tom edged farther into the cave and pressed his back against the cold rock wall.

"Did she put the cufftraps on you when the man gave them to her after you broke things? Did she put them on you ever? Even once?"

"No."

"Of course she didn't. And she won't do it now. That was the man's idea, not hers."

"She doesn't like me."

"She loves you. And you know she loves you."

A shadow cut into the light coming through the cave entrance, and j.b. knew that Tom's mother had reached the clearing on the ledge. He looked out. She stood there in silent silhouette, a shape outlined by the morning sun half risen behind her. Not moving. Aware that her son and the coyote were in the cave, but not knowing what to do. Still thirty steps away. Waiting. Unsure. Alone.

"No, j.b.! There are too many things I can't do!"

"Don't you remember? We all fail. But we hunt again.

We try again. If we quit, the angels can't learn."

Tom said nothing.

A coyote nose touched a boy's hand. j.b. tried once more, "Do you think it might be better to think about the things you *can* do and not so much about the things you *can't* do? Do you think that might be a better way to be?"

A nod. Then a slow hand touched coyote ears. "Yes," said Tom.

With his nipping teeth, j.b. gently clamped onto the edge of Tom's shirt and walked him toward the light.

Mother and son stood looking at each other.

j.b. let go of Tom's shirt and crossed the space to stop near the mother. She knelt down, her eyes still on her boy, and reached out a hand to touch the fur of the wild animal, a hand that asked for hope.

j.b. let her touch the back of his neck, not an easy thing for him to do. But an important thing for him to do.

Tom took one step forward. Then another. And stopped. The boy's eyes stared down at the sand at his feet.

j.b. saw something sparkle on the skin beneath the mother's eyes. The tip of a pink coyote tongue moved and gently touched her skin there, and j.b. tasted the salt of human sorrow.

That small kiss unhitched the mother's doubt. She rushed across white sand and swept the boy into her arms, lifted Tom off the ground, their foreheads touching, their arms around each other, the sounds of joy soft on the morning.

She led Tom down the mountain. j.b. stayed behind.

Tears dry quickly in desert air. All kinds of tears.

As Tom and his mother reached the flatland at the base of Ice Mountain, the sharp crack of a single rifle shot detonated a shimmer of echoes near the south trail.

"Oh, my God," she said. "Hurry, Tom."

Tom turned once to look back up at the cave. He saw j.b. standing in clean light high on the cliff, unmoving, looking south, looking toward the south trail.

Then Tom turned and looked in that direction, too...the trail j.b.'s mother had taken.

Early the next morning Tom and his mother walked to the place of the red stones by the library.

j.b. was not there.

They looked west toward Ice Mountain. Not far away, across a bright reach of early April desert, they saw a young coyote prancing on three legs as he chased sticks and leaves in the sandy skirts of a dust devil spinning through the sage.

Tom's mother knelt down next to her son. "Tom?...Is that...?"

Tom only nodded. Human talk was too hard for him.

In a quiet voice she asked, "I wonder why he's doing

that?" Not expecting an answer.

Tom remembered that he must try. He made the sounds. Human words, at last. "j.b. ...saying goodbye...to an angel."

She turned and stared at him. The shock she felt at hearing him speak gave way to joy, and joy was just as quickly buried by an avalanche of hope. Then she saw his eyes. He was looking at the coyote. She looked at the coyote, too.

Tom's arm went around her shoulder. "But she...will be...again." He tried to make the new words sound brave. Framed by shining tears, what he said spoke more of love than bravery.

He moved close to her side. "I will...tell you...about forever."

In a breath of time no science sees, a thing past faith moved between the mother and her Tom.

They stayed that way for many minutes.
Holding on.
Watching.

End

Timesong

When my days are run,
My angel will know love.
My angel will know trying.
My angel will know how a smile feels,
Beyond the taste of tears.
I promise.

I will…
Bend my shoulder to my brother's rock.
Help my sister climb the hill.
Show my children where the fences are,
Point at possibilities,
…And wish them well.

I will…
Remember that souls move not just on two legs.
That earth must last to teach.
That 'putting back' is the greater part of 'taking.'
That misfortune mastered is the master teacher.
That stars aren't just to wonder at…reach.

When my raindrop returns to the river
My angel will be rich because of me,
Will know about love,
Will know about trying.
Will whisper secrets to God.
…when my days are run.

—**Bill Branon**

Epilogue

The 'Big Bang' theory states that the Universe originated in a singular explosive event. The theory of the Big Bang is widely accepted today. The rate of expansion of the Universe has been measured. Quantum physicists and astronomers are examining the concept that the Universe exists in pulse mode, the oscillating-universe model.

The oscillating-universe theory advances the idea that all matter flying out from the Big Bang origin—stars, planets, interstellar gases, etc.—is being slowed by gravity and will eventually collapse back onto itself only to explode outward again after compressing down to the critical mass that existed at the moment of the Big Bang. The argument hinges on whether the gravitational pull of interstellar matter is sufficient to reverse the expansion that is taking place. If not, the Universe will proceed to the Big Chill, a situation in which all matter keeps expanding outward indefinitely. But if the slowing is sufficient, then the Big Crunch is probable with compression back to singularity.

The collapse back to a singularity was considered as far back as the 1920s when Einstein's math was being examined. But formidable theoretical barriers argued against the probability of another Big Bang recurring to begin the cycle over again. Then, in the early 1990s, the brilliant work of Werner Israel, Eric Poisson, and A. E. Sikkema, while investigating the collapse of black holes, dramatically opened the door to the notion of an oscillating universe. (The reader is referred to Gribbins' book *Unveiling The Edge of Time*, Harmony Books, 1992, pg. 222, et seq.)

To paraphrase some of today's theoreticians: If the Universe does oscillate, if it does recycle, it would be a stretch of ego to suppose that we, today, are in the first cycle of that repetition.

> *"These are real things, Tom. Not make-believe things.*
> *It's numbers...endless time and numbers."*
>
> — j.b.